Water Magic

Mark Jeffrey Stefik

Illustrated by Mark & Barbara Stefik

The Oberlanders: Book 7

The Oberlanders

Published by Portola Publishing
Portola Valley, Ca. 94028 USA

© 2021 by Mark Jeffrey Stefik

Illustrations for the book are by Mark Jeffrey Stefik and Barbara Stefik.

This book is a work of fiction. The characters, incidents, and dialogue are drawn from the author's imagination and are not to be construed as real. Any resemblance to actual events or persons, living or dead, is entirely coincidental.

Water Magic the seventh book in *The Oberlanders*. The books describe fictional events in a universe including the planets Sol #3 and Zorcon.

Further information about the series can be found at www.PortolaPublishing.com

Library of Congress Cataloging-in-Publication Data
Copyright Office Registration Number:
Stefik, Mark Jeffrey
   Water Magic / Mark Jeffrey Stefik
Edition 3
ISBN: 978-1-943176-17-5

The Fairy Godmother gleefully promised Santa's bored Elves a mountain for their ski resort at the North Pole. It was just one more Good Deed. Perhaps it would restore the planetary anthropologist's reputation. Meanwhile, Hansel, Gretel, BC and Charley took Marie's new household android on an adventure to an alpine lake. The kids, the androids, and Cinderwan were all startled when a water beast rose from the lake and roared. More was at stake than Cinderwan realized when she began wielding her new Elder powers.

Books in *The Oberlanders*

Magic with Side Effects (#1)

Magic Misspoken (#2)

Old Magic Awakens (#3)

Magic Reprogrammed (#4)

Earth Magic (#5)

Fire Magic (#6)

Water Magic (#7)

Air Magic (#8)

Space and Time Magic (#9)

The Sendroids series continues after *The Oberlanders*. Information about both series can be found on the website www.PortolaPublishing.com

ACKNOWLEDGMENTS

Thank you to our wonderful friends and early readers who read earlier versions of the folktales of *The Oberlanders* as we developed them. Special thanks to Asli Aydin, Phil Berghausen, Eric and Emma Bier, Danny Bobrow, J.J. and Stu Card, Nilesh and Laura Doctor, Ollie Eggiman, Lance Good, Craig Heberer, Chris Kavert, Ray and Lois Kuntz, Raj and Zoe Minhas, Ranjeeta Prakash, Mary Ann Puppo, Jamie Richard, Lynne Russell, Mali Sarpangal, Jackie Shek, Morgan Stefik, Sebastian Steiger, Frank Torres, Paige Turner, Blanca Vargas, Barry and Joyce Vissell, Alan and Pam Wu, Meili Xu, and their kids and young relatives.

Thank you also to the people of Gimmelwald and Mürren, Switzerland in the Swiss Alps and the people of Vetan in Valle d'Aosta in the Italian Alps. These places inspired us with their natural beauty and stillness, and the power of the mountains, lakes, forests, and waterfalls. The people of the Alps have histories and traditions that reach back into legend and folktale.

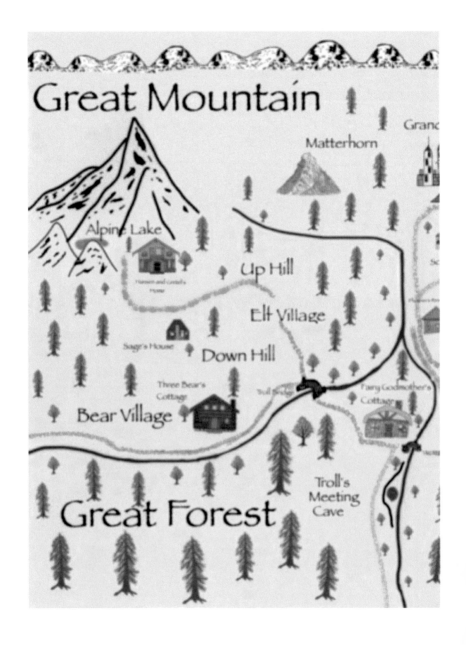

Water Magic

CONTENTS

Water Magic

"After my Cookie Machine left my service to join the natives, Professor Grimmicus suggested that I get another android to help around the cottage." *Sol #3 Council Debriefings of Planetary Anthropologist Marie GottMothercus* recorded by Stuarticus Cardicus, Declassified Archives of the Zorcon Empire.

Water Magic

1 A Hurried Departure

The air whistled as Elfin James banked Santa's sleigh for a landing. The reindeer brought the sleigh down in the meadow by the Fairy Godmother's cottage.

Elfin James checked the reindeer.

"It will be fun to hang out with you and Luke again," said Goldilocks to her brother after they landed from their quick flight from Elf Village. "And it will be great to see all the toymakers and the toys for next Christmas!"

"Um," hesitated James. "The toys that we have in production are 'top secret.' You know the drill. We're still working on new designs," he added, "and lists have to be made."

"How is everybody doing?" she asked.

"We work all of the time," James began. "Some of the elves are getting restless. Skiing is no good. The North Pole is too flat. But that may change soon."

"Why is that?" asked Goldilocks.

"The Fairy Godmother says that she can put a mountain at the pole," he said. "Everyone is excited about that. That's why she's coming up there again."

James got out to check on the reindeer. It would be a few minutes before they would leave.

The Fairy Godmother came out from her cottage to the sleigh. Her real name was Marie Gottmothercus. Her friends called her Marie. Most people in Oberland Kingdom, including Goldilocks, knew her as the Fairy Godmother. For them she was a kindly lady who usually kept to herself. It was rumored that she occasionally did Good Deeds.

Marie and Goldilocks settled in their seat and talked.

The villagers did not know that she was a planetary anthropologist from Zorcon or that her "magic wand" was a matter-antimatter long-range model-3 transputer. It used computers, nanotechnology, and energy channeled from Zorcon.

Following a suggestion from Professor Grimmicus, Marie created a new android a few days earlier. It was a Multi-Talented Apparatus. Unlike her first android, this one looked like a young native woman. The android was helping her around the cottage.

The android was expected to answer the door and to greet visitors. Nobody had visited so far. She was supposed to make visitors comfortable. However, she was not to provide information about Zorcon or the Fairy Godmother's business. She was also to report back to the Zorcon Library and Professor Grimmicus about any anomalies she observed on Sol #3.

The android looked out the cottage window at the sleigh. Checking with the Zorcon University Library, she learned that Santa flew this sleigh on Christmas Eve to deliver toys to children around the world. The sleigh did not look like other historic flying vehicles in the library. It was pulled by reindeer. Its flight physics were unknown.

"Let's rock and roll!"

Marie and Goldilocks settled into a seat on the sleigh and talked. Before Marie took over the real estate office in Elf Village, Marie had bought her cottage from Goldilocks' father, Elfin John.

Looking out from the cottage window, the android adjusted her hearing so that she could hear their conversation.

Goldilocks asked, "If you can put a mountain at the North Pole to create a ski-area, couldn't you also put a ski mountain in Oberland

Kingdom? It would be great if people could ski closer to Elf Village!"

The android consulted the library records on planetary anthropology. Creating a mountain was a significant energy expense and unusual for a planetary anthropologist. Planetary anthropologists were drilled in the rule to "Listen, Learn, and Leave it Alone." Creating mountains was not "leaving things alone." Marie's plan was an anomaly. However, the android had only been instructed to report on anomalies of Sol #3.

Just then James pulled on the reins and shouted, "Let's rock and roll!" to the reindeer. The reindeer leaned forward and rapidly pulled the sleigh up in the air.

The branch crashed through the window!

Just down the road a young woman, a young man, a young bear, and a metallic man were on their way to the cottage with a basket of cookies for the Fairy Godmother.

With his sharp sight, Charley was the first to see Santa's sleigh racing skywards. He pointed it out to Hansel, BC, and Gretel.

Hansel smiled, "It's James, showing off again!"

The sleigh turned sharply. It passed close to a tree by the Fairy Godmother's cottage, causing the tree to sway in its wake.

The sleigh blurred with speed. Hansel, BC, and Gretel were startled as a loud boom reached them. Charley's blue eye flashed and his red eye flashed. "That sleigh is flying faster than 767 miles per hour," he announced.

"That's a lot faster than I thought reindeer could fly," grinned Hansel.

BC snorted. Reindeer couldn't normally fly. The young bear knew that magic was involved.

Charley knew that the sleigh did not operate by normal flying principles, but he was used to it. He had seen other unusual things on Sol #3.

"Did you see who was on the sleigh?" asked Gretel.

Charley blinked. "Besides James," he said, "the Fairy Godmother and Goldilocks."

"If the Fairy Godmother is away, what should we do with the cookies?" asked BC. "Sage told us to give the cookies to her."

"I can think of one or two things we might do with them," answered Hansel slyly.

Just then there was a loud crack as a high branch broke off the swaying tree. It bounced, twisted, and tumbled down towards the Fairy Godmother's cottage. The branch crashed right through the round window.

The branch struck the android. It knocked her to the kitchen floor. She skidded backwards, breaking her sandals.

"Oof!" she said, as she bumped against the kitchen counter.

Charley exclaimed, "There is trouble at the cottage!"

"It sounded like someone was hurt," added Gretel.

"Let's hurry," shouted Hansel, running to the cottage ahead of the others.

2 Emma Chooses Adventure

he four young people ran to the cottage. Hansel was about to open the door and dash in when Gretel touched his shoulder and gave him a look.

"Remember last time," she cautioned.

A disheveled young woman answered the door.

BC stepped up to the door and knocked.

They heard the shuffle of footsteps approaching. The door opened. A disheveled young woman looked out.

Gretel stepped forward and handed her the basket of cookies. She said, "Sage sent us with these cookies for the Fairy Godmother."

"Hello," she said. "I'm sorry, but the Fairy Godmother is not at home now."

"Oh, thank you," said the young woman. The android consulted the library about Sage's cookies. She answered politely, "The Fairy Godmother enjoys Sage's cookies."

The travelers saw that she had a blue eye and a red eye. Her blue eye flashed.

The android looked at the visitors. There was a young woman and a young man. There was a young member of the Ursidae family (Bears), wearing clothing and talking with the others. Her blue eye flashed and her red eye flashed again.

Outside were a young woman, a young man, an android, and what seemed to be a bear wearing clothing.

The library had no record of bears wearing clothes or talking, except in ancient folktales. Perhaps this was a person in a costume. The Multi-Talented Apparatus examined the young bear more closely. It was not a person in a costume. It was a real bear. A talking bear was an anomaly. She queued this anomaly in her communications system for transmission and analysis by the Zorcon University Library.

The young people introduced themselves.

"I'm Gretel," said the young woman.

"I'm BC," said the young bear.

"I'm Hansel," said the young man.

Then she looked at the fourth "person." He was mostly titanium. He looked like a model 67 mobile general-purpose apparatus, except that he wore clothing and had hair. He did not act like an android. He interacted with the others like a person.

Charley bowed. "I'm Charley," he said.

Again, her blue eye blinked and her red eye blinked. She used her wireless communications system to send him a message. The message said, "I am a Multi-Talented Model 117 Home Appliance, identification AB97130-M38572245. What is your identification? What is your purpose?"

Charley smiled when he received the wireless message. His wireless communication system was operational, but it was now completely under his conscious control. Charley spoke out loud and did not respond wirelessly.

"Hi," said Charley. "My purpose is to live, learn, and do right things, I think."

"My purpose is to live, learn, and do right things, I think."

The red and blue eyes of the Multi-Talented Apparatus blinked again. She checked her library. There was no record of any android still on Sol #3. A Cookie Machine android had been there, but it had been broken. There was no record of an android that did not automatically identify itself with an appliance identifier. There was no record of an android having the purpose to "live, learn, and do right things". This was another anomaly.

She spoke to everyone. She said, "I am a Multi-Talented Apparatus. My purpose is to do housekeeping and other errands for the Fairy Godmother."

"Hmm," said BC. Calling the girl a Multi-Talented Apparatus would be pretty awkward. His parents had named him Christopher Bear, but everyone had called him Baby Bear for a long time. When he had outgrown that name, Hansel called him by his initials, but reversing their order. Now his friends called him "BC" He liked the "BC" nickname. They should give the 'Multi-Talented Apparatus a nickname. "We could call her 'M.A.'," suggested BC.

Gretel smiled. "Her name is *Emma*," she said with great authority. She had taken on the role of naming appliances.

"Emma!" said Hansel, approvingly.

"Emma!" said BC, smiling.

"Emma!" said Charley. He had been learning about politeness at Oberland School, so he added, "That's a lovely name."

"Her name is Emma!"

The Multi-Talented Apparatus blinked again. The young people had proposed to give her a short name. Naming of androids was common since humans do not like to remember long names. However, the owner or master usually assigned the name. Marie Gottmothercus had not yet given her a name. The android checked the library. Occasionally other people assigned temporary names to androids. Such a naming practice was permissible.

"I can answer to 'Emma'," she said accepting the nickname.

Gretel looked at Emma. Emma's speech was awkward.

Gretel asked, "Emma. Are you hurt? We heard a branch crash down. It seems to have hit you."

Emma's blue eye blinked. "I am undamaged. It would take more than a tree branch to damage me."

Emma heard noises in the kitchen and saw that Hansel, BC, and Charley were repairing the damaged window. BC had picked up the branch and was carrying it to the yard. Hansel swept the tree debris from the floor. Charley arranged the pieces of broken glass. He moved his hand over the cracks as he reassembled and repaired the window. His finger glowed brightly. Charley was skillfully mending the broken glass.

Emma had never seen anyone repair something before. Usually, broken things were just replaced. She had never seen an android work with a group of people. Her blue eye blinked and her red eye blinked.

"Look," Gretel smiled, "The boys are repairing the window!"

"The boys are repairing the window."

Emma did not know what to say. In her experience, people did not thank androids and people did not fix things. Nor did bears. The library suggested that the best response was, "Thank you," but androids were usually not expected to give thanks. Emma offered, "The Fairy Godmother will probably be grateful." She said 'probably' because it was not completely certain *what* the Fairy Godmother would say about all this.

Gretel thought that "probably" was an odd thing to say. She looked at Emma curiously.

BC snorted. "And we'll *probably* be grateful that she is probably grateful," he said.

Hansel smiled. "And I'd *probably* be grateful for a glass of water," he added.

Charley's blue eye blinked and his red eye blinked. "This glass repair is making me hungry. I'd *probably* be grateful for something to eat."

Gretel frowned at the boys. "I'd *definitely* be grateful if boys remembered when they were guests and were politer," she said.

Hansel grinned, "Yeah. It's nice to be nice."

BC elaborated, "It's nice to be nice to the nice."

Charley's blue eye blinked. He added, "*Probably.*"

Emma and Gretel got the cookies and milk together.

Gretel started to frown, but instead she laughed and soon everyone was laughing. Emma did not understand laughing. She noticed that Charley was laughing. Emma considered laughing, but androids don't laugh. It was confusing.

Then Gretel suggested to Emma, "Perhaps we could prepare something for the boys to eat."

Except for the cookies and some milk, there was no food in the cottage. Usually when the Fairy Godmother wanted food or anything else, she created it with her wand. Emma asked, "Would cookies and milk be satisfactory?"

"Things are looking up," said BC. All the boys brightened and sat at the kitchen table. Emma and Gretel got the cookies and milk together. Gretel ate some cookies too. Charley ate too. An android eating was an anomaly. Emma reported it to the Zorcon University library. She didn't eat anything.

Afterwards, Gretel said to Emma, "Perhaps you and I could freshen up while the boys clean the kitchen."

Gretel and Emma then went off. When they were alone, Gretel observed, "You may not be damaged," she said, "but your clothing is dusty, and your shoes are a wreck."

Emma looked down at her clothing and shoes. "The Fairy Godmother can replace them when she returns in a few days," she said, deciding not to say more about it.

"Do you have another pair of shoes?" asked Gretel.

Emma shook her head. "I have only needed one pair to do my work around the cottage," she said.

"Could you use a nice pair of boots?"

Gretel stood proudly. "My father is the best woodcarver in the kingdom and also an excellent shoemaker. You could use a nice pair of boots to wear when you go shopping," she added.

Emma's blue eye blinked. She consulted the library. 'Shopping' was something that people on Zorcon used to do before assembly nano-bots were invented. People on Sol #3 probably still shopped. She had no instructions about shopping.

"I have no instructions about shopping," she said simply,

The library showed that women often had several pairs of shoes. "I have not needed more shoes yet since I have been here only for a few days," she answered.

Gretel continued. "Then you must come with us to our home. My father can make you a fine pair of boots. Emma's blue eye blinked and her red eye blinked. The library had no information about people making clothing for androids. Appliances like her were constructed with clothing and could occasionally arrange for replacement. "Perhaps," she said uncertainly.

Emma thought about leaving the cottage with the others. The Fairy Godmother had not instructed her not to leave. But Emma had a secondary assignment to observe anomalies and to report them back to the Zorcon University Library, attention to Professor Grimmicus.

Gretel took her hand. "Then it's settled." Gretel then helped Emma clean her dress and make temporary repairs to her sandals.

"This will probably be acceptable," said Emma.

Afterwards, the group of travelers including Emma locked up the Fairy Godmother's Cottage and started hiking to Hansel and Gretel's home.

3 A Simple Life

organ sat with Cinderella on a bench by the sea. Jorgan tried to engage Cinderella in conversation.

He said, "These have been busy days. I met the dragons before they flew off to Amerland this morning and thanked them for the ride to Hawaii."

Cinderella nodded. She asked, "How was Gabby?"

King Jorgan thanked the dragons for bringing them to Hawaii.

Gabby was a departing Master at Oberland School. Besides watching over the students and teaching classes, Gabby would be an ambassador for Oberland during the bi-mester.

Jorgan responded, "She is excited as usual. She talked about teaching Science and Pragmatics. She is planning an intense program for the students."

Cinderella nodded. She did not seem to be paying much attention.

"I have been thinking about my father," Jorgan continued. "King Morgan did not seem to age. He seemed as young when he left on his journey as he was when I was a child."

He let the thought hang, but Cinderella said nothing.

"It is possible that he is an Elder," he continued. "Before he left, he said that in our reign there would be 'a great nexus in the time flow'."

Cinderella looked up. "That could explain why he abdicated when he was so young. Elders have very long-term concerns. As an Elder, it would be unusual for him to sustain an interest in the daily running of a kingdom."

Jorgan looked at Cinderella carefully. "And yet you have been very involved in running our kingdom. You make a difference in everything." He let the thought linger.

"I just wanted a simple life as a princess and a queen."

Cinderella was still preoccupied with her own thoughts. Jorgan waited.

Cinderella looked up, sighed, and smiled at him. As always, his heart lifted when he saw her smile. "So much is happening, Jorgan," she started. Jorgan nodded.

"The ancients are stirred up. They are rushing my training and testing me with urgency," she sighed. "I just wanted a simple life as a princess and a queen."

Jorgan tried to hide his smile. "A 'simple life' as a princess and a queen!" he laughed.

Cinderella realized what she had said and laughed too. There was nothing simple about being a princess or a queen.

She continued, "I worry that my Elder training will take me away from you, my love. I know that this is not just about me, or even about us. I wanted to expand my horizons in a bigger world, but I never wished this Elder business for my life."

Jorgan felt sadness in his heart. He had sensed much the same possibility. He breathed to release his pain.

"Rulers and Elders have duties beyond their simple lives. We must embrace our time together," he said. "We have our moments together, but we do not know the count of them."

4 Water Sprites

he Phoenix ran up to Jorgan and Cinderella.

He had regrown to his former size. He had also regained his memories by studying with the Scholar.

The Phoenix clicked and chirped in agitation. Cinderwan found that she was understanding him better. "Elder training cannot be rushed," grumbled the Phoenix. "Especially at this time, *proper* training is crucial."

"Elder training cannot be rushed!"

"What is special about this time?" wondered Cinderella.

The Phoenix muttered, "The future is not completely predictable. These times are chaotic."

Cinderella felt a few sprinkles of rain. She looked skywards but there were no rain clouds overhead. She turned to Jorgan. He was wiping some drops from his face. They heard giggling in the trees behind them.

Suddenly the Phoenix spread his wings and flew up into a palm tree. There was a chorus of "Hey" and he flew back down carrying two small green boys with yellow wings. The water sprites argued and protested.

The Phoenix had two green boys with yellow wings.

The boys held little plant bulbs with stems. The rain sprinkles were the result of their trickster play, not Hawaiian rain.

The Phoenix dropped the water sprites on the beach near King Jorgan and Queen Cinderella.

"Aha," said Jorgan, smiling.

The Phoenix clicked and chirped some more. Then Cinderwan noticed the water bulbs.

"Hmm. Is this the source of the rain?" she asked.

"Oh, oh," said one of the boys stepping backwards.

The other boy straightened and spoke. "Thistle sent us," he declared. "She is coming soon to meet with Cinderwan."

"She will request that Cinderwan go with her," added the other, running around.

"You may get wet!" said the first boy.

"So, in our way, we were delivering our message," said the second boy, trying to sound convincing.

The Phoenix swished a wing over the boys' heads and they both ducked. Everyone laughed.

"Thank you, Niner," said Cinderella, smiling.

"Is this the source of the rain?"

"And thank you for the message," said Cinderella to the water sprite boys. She sighed. The upcoming meeting had to be about her next training.

"And what are your names, my water-bearing messengers?" she asked. The boys giggled.

"I'm Petal," said the first water sprite.

"I'm Petal."

"I'm Leaf," said the second one, as he ran back from the sea.

"It's nice to meet you," said Cinderella. She looked to Jorgan. "I will prepare to meet Thistle," she said.

5 Home Sweet Home

he young people walked on a forest path above Elf Village to Hansel's and Gretel's family chalet. Hansel, BC, and Charley led the way. Gretel and Emma followed.

Gretel tried to engage Emma in conversation. "How long have you been with the Fairy Godmother?" she asked.

Emma's blue eye flashed. "This is my third day," she answered.

"This is my third day."

"Do you like it here?" asked Gretel.

Emma's blue eye flashed. She searched the library for android responses to Gretel's question. There were no examples of people asking androids whether they 'liked' something.

Emma replied, "I am not sure how to answer you."

Gretel was puzzled. Her question 'Do you like it here?' was not difficult. Gretel tried again, "Where have you been before?"

Emma answered. "Working for the Fairy Godmother is my first

assignment."

Apparently, Emma had very little practice in conversation. Gretel asked, "Do you talk with the Fairy Godmother?"

"The Fairy Godmother tells me what to do," replied Emma.

"That doesn't sound like much fun," commented Gretel.

Emma consulted the library for examples of "fun." Her chores did not match examples of fun. "That's probably true," she said.

"What do you do for fun?" asked Gretel.

Emma considered the question. Having fun was not one of her responsibilities. She replied, "I just wait." Then she added, "This is my first time away from the cottage."

"Well, then!" said Gretel. "There are lots of *fun* things we can show you." She continued. "Would you like that?"

Emma remembered her assignment to report anomalies to the Zorcon University Library. If Gretel and the others showed her fun things, there would be more to report. "That would be acceptable," she replied.

Emma consulted the library again. She found that after young women say something, they often smile. Emma smiled.

Just then they entered a clearing in the woods. A chalet sat back in the clearing. "Home sweet home!" exclaimed Hansel.

"Home sweet home."

Emma consulted the library. In situations like this, young women often used a standard phrase. She said, "What a lovely home!"

Gretel turned to Emma in surprise. Emma had volunteered an opinion! "Thank you," said Gretel. But something did not make sense to her. "I am curious, Emma. May I ask you a question?"

"Try and stop her!" suggested Hansel slyly.

Gretel rolled her eyes and flashed Hansel a look.

BC and Charley laughed. Hansel could be funny.

Emma considered Gretel's question and Hansel's suggestion to stop Gretel. Stopping Gretel would be inappropriate.

Emma smiled and replied, "I will try to answer."

Gretel continued. "This is your first time away from the Fairy Godmother's cottage, right?"

Emma nodded.

"You probably haven't seen many homes. How did you decide that our chalet is lovely?" asked Gretel.

"How did you decide that our chalet is lovely?"

Charley realized that Gretel's question was unexpected. Emma would not know what to say. Charley had practiced talking with Hansel, BC, and others. He had also engaged in many conversations at the Oberland School. Emma needed help.

Charley offered, "Perhaps Emma was looking at the symmetry in the home design. Many of its proportions follow the Golden Rule. Also, its colors are well balanced." He had learned rules about beauty in his classes in Theory and Pragmatics at Oberland School.

Now BC was puzzled. He asked, "Where would Emma learn about theories of beauty? We shouldn't ask so many questions of someone we just met!"

Hansel and Gretel felt that way too. Then Hansel smiled and said, "Our father, Geppetto, designs shoes and chalets. He uses the Golden Rule in his designs!"

Emma's red eye flashed and her blue eye flashed. The others were putting words to ideas. Her libraries contained many concepts. Maybe she could use concepts from the library to help her answer questions. It showed that a young woman typically said, 'Thank you!' when someone helped. On the other hand, people did not usually thank androids and Charley was an android.

Turning to the others, Emma said, "Thank you, Charley. I tried to answer Gretel's question, but I was at a loss for words."

Emma smiled. Then she added, "Anyway, I could probably use a nice pair of boots!"

Gretel smiled back. With more practice in conversation, Emma might almost sound normal.

6 The Beast Roars

s the children walked to the chalet, Emma thought back to her first moments awakening in Marie Gottmothercus' kitchen. The Fairy Godmother had muttered, "Grimmicus must think that I need a 'Cinderella' appliance." Emma opened her eyes.

"Grimmicus must think that I need a 'Cinderella' appliance."

Marie gave Emma instructions about keeping house and running errands. She told Emma to use brooms, dusters, and buckets of soapy water. According to the library, brooms and dusters had not been used for cleaning homes on Zorcon for hundreds of years. She did not say anything about that.

Marie's kitchen had an ancient pot that could be hung in the fireplace for cooking. However, Marie never cooked and rarely shopped. She used her wand to create meals. "Too much bother to cook," she would say.

Marie did not like doing things the hard way, like the natives of Sol #3. She used her wand to ease the rigors of primitive living.

Marie also did not chop wood for her fireplace. The flames in her fireplace were real and the wood was real. However, the flames burned gas that was materialized by a Zorcon transputer and the logs never needed replacing. A thin layer of cold inert gas separated the gas flames from the logs.

Marie especially liked some things about Sol #3. Marie loved her cookies and her tea. She liked the old style of clothing. And she especially liked her boots.

An ancient pot for cooking sat by the fireplace.

Emma was still reflecting on Marie and her boots when Geppetto offered her a choice of boots to replace her broken sandals "You can have boots like any you see here!" he offered. "Or I could make you something more to your fancy."

Gretel gave an opinion. "Papa – could you start with a black pair and add dyed leather strips to match Emma's clothing?"

"Certainly!" said Geppetto. A few hours later he presented Emma with new boots.

"Do you like these?" he asked Emma.

The boots felt soft on Emma's feet. They would keep her feet clean. Emma nodded. She could learn to "like" them.

Emma reported about her new boots to the Zorcon University Library. The library requested details about the boot design. Emma was not sure why the library wanted to know about that. She did not expect that other androids on Zorcon would soon be wearing boots.

"You can have boots like any that you see here."

Geppetto wanted to check on matters at Alpine Lake. Recently there had been stories about strange happenings there. And Geppetto wanted to go fishing.

Emma could learn to "like" her new boots.

They set off for Alpine Lake. When they arrived, they got into a rowboat boat and rowed into the lake.

Emma looked over the water. Just as she turned a beast raised its head. It had been below the water. It was about a mile away. The beast looked at them. Its eyes got big and it opened its mouth.

Everyone heard the roar a few seconds later. The beast swam towards them.

The beast raised its head.

Geppetto looked at it and said, "Oh-oh." He pointed to a cave by a cliff. "I am not sure what that beast is, but we had better get to that cave before it reaches us! Paddle quickly, everyone!"

Everyone heard the loud roar.

Emma checked the library. There were no records of large beasts on lakes on Sol #3 or Zorcon. This was an anomaly. And it might be dangerous.

7 Thistle

 water sprite woman stepped out from the waterfalls. Petal and Leaf came with her. Her clothing was made of woven vines. She had transparent light blue wings with yellow ribs and wore a flowery yellow cap that looked like the top of a thistle.

A water sprite woman stepped from the waterfalls.

The woman bowed. "I am Thistle," she announced.

Noticing the Phoenix, she bowed to him. "I am honored to see you, again," she smiled. Then she turned to Cinderwan and Jorgan.

"I am pleased to meet you, Cinderwan," she said, "And you, King Jorgan, son of Morgan."

Cinderwan and Jorgan bowed. Cinderwan reached out with her senses to Thistle. She heard a heartbeat, but it had a constant and unvarying rhythm. She heard Thistle's breathing, but Thistle's exhale did not change in temperature or content from her inhale. Cinderwan also sensed where Thistle's feet touched the ground. There was a slight watery flow back and forth. Thistle was no regular water sprite.

"I am deeply honored, Elder Thistle of the Water Element," said Cinderella, bowing again.

As she answered, Cinderwan felt a ripple of time flex around her. Thistle had stopped time. The others had not heard Cinderwan's greeting. Thistle spoke to Cinderwan in the deep tones of a bell ringing underwater.

"For most of your training you will live in the sea."

"I am here to train you and also to test you, Cinderwan of the Earth and Fire Elements," answered Thistle.

"Your enhanced senses suggest that you have talent for Water Element training," intoned Thistle. "Your element trainings have been rushed. I wonder whether you are ready for the Water Element. This training requires patience, testing, and time.

Thistle continued, "Mastering the Water Element requires reflecting on who you are and deepening the integrity of your identity. Your will live in the sea and learn about life in the flow. Water is essential for life. There is much more for you to experience, Cinderwan."

Cinderella bowed again. "I am not sure that I am ready," she answered.

"No one ever is," said Thistle smiling. "You will take several forms in training with me. We will spend whatever time is needed."

"I will start time again and so that we can talk with the others before we start your training.

Cinderwan bowed again. "Thank you, Thistle," she said. As she said it, she felt time start up again.

Thistle turned to Jorgan and the others. "I will take Cinderwan to her training. She will rejoin you later in Oberland."

8 Seeking Refuge in a Cave

veryone pushed on the oars. They had almost reached the shore.

The water beast was closing in on them. They needed to get inside the cave.

Hansel and Gretel helped Geppetto walk to the cave.

As they jumped out of the boat, Geppetto tripped and hurt his leg. Now he was limping. Hansel and Gretel helped him walk to the cave.

BC yanked a boulder from the beach. He heaved it into the air, striking the approaching beast on its head. The beast staggered and fell back into the water. "Run," he shouted to Charley and Emma.

Charley stood firm. "You get to the cave," he said, "Block the entrance with boulders. I will delay the beast while you protect the others."

Charley grabbed a branch in a pile of leaves. He focused. A finger on his hand turned white hot. He touched the leaves and they burst into flames.

Grabbing the flaming branch Charley advanced towards the water beast, as it rose again out of the water.

BC and Emma ran to the cave. Charley waved the flaming branch to distract the beast. The water beast swung its powerful tail through the air, aiming at Charley. Charley leaped aside barely avoiding it. The ground shook as the tail pounded the beach.

Charley distracted the beast with a flaming branch.

Slowly, Charley retreated towards the cave. He lifted boulders lying on the beach and started throwing them in a barrage at the beast. The boulders struck the beast and partly buried it. The beast roared.

Suddenly Charley felt weak. He was exhausted from igniting branches and heaving boulders. He staggered towards the cave. The glow faded from his eyes and his vision shrank to a tiny dot. Charley collapsed a few feet from the cave.

When Charley collapsed, the beast turned away from him and started walking towards the cave.

BC had blocked the entrance with boulders. He peaked out and saw Charley. BC squeezed through a small opening. He growled and heaved a heavy rock at the beast. The beast staggered backwards down the hill. Then BC scrambled over to Charley and dragged him to the small opening.

The others were inside. Emma and BC grabbed Charley's hands. The ground shook as the beast approached the cave entrance. Just in time his friends pulled Charley into the cave. Charley was still.

The water beast peered through the opening. Then it reached through the opening with one of its clawed legs.

The water beast peered in.

Emma faced the beast. She flexed her right arm. The metal of her arm flowed as she reshaped it into a titanium blade.

BC's eyes got big. He had seen Charley change the shape of his arm, but he did not realize that Emma could do that too. "Wow!" was all he could say.

Planting her feet firmly on the ground Emma shouted, "Not today, Beastie! You will not hurt these people!" Emma swung her blade arm and struck the beast's leg. The blade sliced deep into the beast's leg. The beast roared and pulled back its leg. They heard shaking and howling and stomping outside.

Gretel stared at Emma. What was happening to that shy girl who barely said anything in conversation? Although Emma looked like a human girl, Gretel had known that she was an android like Charley. She looked like a girl, but she was made of titanium. There was more to Emma than they had realized.

Emma swung her blade arm.

When the beast withdrew, Emma shook her arm for a second. It flowed back to its original arm shape. She also relaxed and shifted back to her calm and reserved manner.

Just then there was a rustling sound in the cave. A pile of mud and straw was moving and making noises. Something alive was in the cave with them.

9 The Field Test

inderwan and Thistle faced the sea. Thistle suggested, "Reach out with your mind. Can you sense your kingdom in the east?"

Cinderwan reached out. Her fire magic sharpened her senses. She saw the Great Mountain and the Alpine Lake above Elf Village.

Cinderwan saw a beast outside the cave.

She felt a disturbance near Alpine Lake. People in a cave were in danger.

BC had blocked the cave entrance with boulders. Geppetto was inside with an injured ankle. Hansel and Gretel were there too. Charley was there, but his inner light was very dim. There was also a girl made of titanium. She was communicating with Zorcon.

Outside the cave a water beast was pacing. It had an injured leg. It raged and pushed boulders away from the cave entrance.

This was not permissible in her kingdom! Attacking her people was not okay. Heat rose in Cinderwan. She would restore order in her kingdom.

"My Kingdom! My rules!" she growled.

She reached out with her mind and projected herself to the cave.

A column of water rose noisily out of the lake. It took the form of a hooded warrior woman. The water glowed red with flickering flames as Cinderwan materialized. Her warrior eyes glowed with fiery fury.

"My kingdom! My rules!"

"Step away from that cave!" commanded Cinderwan. Cinderwan was terrifying in her fury.

The beast growled at her.

Cinderwan materialized a golden staff in her hand. She spoke, "I claim and rule this kingdom."

Cinderwan struck her staff to the ground. A shudder rolled through Oberland Kingdom as the land responded to her claiming. Cinderwan had not yet trained to this level, but in her fury, she had invoked a high level of Earth and Fire Magic.

The earth shook even in Hawaii. King Jorgan's eyes widened as he felt the claiming in Oberland. The Elves felt it as an earthquake close at hand. The Noble houses shook. Several dragons flew into the air to investigate.

Papa Bear felt the tremor where he stood in the forest. His eyes flashed yellow and he glowed with Earth magic. He looked to Alpine Lake and saw BC in a cave. He saw the water beast.

Papa Bear whispered, "Cinderwan. You are in over your head."

"I claim this kingdom."

This was a serious matter. Papa Bear growled. He looked towards the Great Mountain and started to grow.

Cinderwan struck her staff on the water. The water beast still did not retreat. She was still drawing on powers loaned by Thistle. Cinderwan commanded, "I call on the power of the Water Element!"

A wave rose and swept the beast to the middle of Alpine Lake. Cinderwan stomped after it. She grew taller with every step. Cinderwan became a formidable giant. She whirled her staff and spun a tornado of water around the beast. The water beast dropped in the whirlpool to the bottom of the lake.

Sage turned towards Alpine Lake and felt the whirlpool. Her eyes flashed yellow. An Elder battle had been called. Cinderwan had invoked borrowed Water Magic. She was not yet properly trained in the Water Element and yet she had commanded the water in the lake. Sage saw the water beast at the lake bottom. She felt Cinderwan's rage. The beast felt familiar to her, somehow.

Cinderwan's eyes glowed with fire. The beast sat in the vortex at the bottom of the lake. "I call on the power of Fire," called out Cinderwan. Fire and lightning sparked from her staff and thunder echoed off the mountains.

In Hawaii, Mama Bear felt Cinderwan's Fire Magic. Her eyes flashed yellow. Cinderwan was commanding Earth, Water, and Fire Magic. Steam swirled around Cinderwan. Cinderwan was invoking Elder battle. Mama

Bear saw the water beast crouched at the bottom of the lake. She saw Cinderwan's rage and watched her fury rise. Cinderwan intended to roast the beast in flames of fire.

Papa Bear began to glow with Earth Magic.

Mama Bear saw that fire energy was driving Cinderwan's fury. Cinderwan was lost in her power.

The water beast was pulled into the whirlpool.

Elder Mama Bear closed her eyes and raised her hands in prayer. She knew that Cinderella had lost her mother as a young girl. So much responsibility had been placed on her. Perhaps Cinderwan's Fire Element training had been too rushed. Mama Bear sang out the Máthair ag Glaoch invocation with all of her heart.

> Mothers of daughters
> Power and fear
> A daughter is storming
> Please hold her dear.

"Mothers of daughters ... Please hold her dear."

Her invocation rippled across Sol #3. Calming waves rippled across Earth. It rippled across time. It rippled across the metaverse.

In just that moment Cinderwan's mother, Bodiwan, embraced Cinderwan. She whispered, "When you lose focus on the Stillness, breathe deeply."

Cinderwan paid no attention. She was engaged in righteous battle and intended to restore order. The water swirled and the heat from her staff intensified. Cinderwan raised her staff. Lightning flashed and thunder cracked.

Emma peered out and watched the spectacle in the lake. This was a major anomaly. She sent an anomaly alert to Zorcon. The image of the rising warrior woman went to the Zorcon University Library. The anomaly alert went to Professor Grimmicus.

Bodiwan whispered a second time to Cinderwan. "When you lose focus on the Silence, listen deeply."

Cinderwan's mother's face flickered in her mind. Cinderwan noticed that she was out of balance. She breathed slowly. Her rage began to subside.

"When you lose focus on the Stillness, breathe deeply."

Bodiwan embraced her daughter and whispered a third time. "When you lose focus on the Spaciousness, see deeply. The Stillness, Silence, and Spaciousness are always there for you, my daughter. Return to your inner refuge."

Cinderwan looked into the beast's eyes and saw its fear. She felt its desperation. The water beast was a mother. The beast mother feared for the safety of her child. Cinderwan paused and understood. Her fury subsided.

As Cinderwan stilled her mind, the lake settled into a smooth mirror.

Fire faded from Cinderwan's eyes. Her staff cooled. She raised her hand and raised a circle of land beneath the water beast. Cinderwan touched the beast's wounded leg and healed it. The beast mother felt Cinderwan's compassion and relaxed.

Cinderwan called to the group in the cave. "There is a beast baby in the cave with you. Please comfort and care for it."

Just then a little red beasty head peaked out from a pile of straw and mud back in the cave. Hansel, Gretel, BC, Geppetto, and Emma looked at it. Gretel smiled.

The commotion outside had subsided. The beast stopped worrying about its baby. It sat down and waited.

BC began moving the boulders away from the cave entrance. Everyone prepared to go outside. BC and Emma carried Charley out and sat him down. Charley's energy was returning. He stirred. His eyes flickered and he looked around.

Hansel and Gretel played with the baby.

Hansel and Gretel played with the baby, who smiled at its mother. Gretel brushed mud gently from the baby. She was cooing with the baby and brushed away some straw. The baby liked the attention and snuggled Gretel.

Seeing that things were calming down, Hansel grinned. He looked at the mud and straw and made up a poem.

> There once was a Lady named Ness
> Whose cave was a terrible mess.
> She put Baby Red
> In a mud-and-grass bed, saying
> More work is harder than less.

BC laughed, "Lazy beast mom!"

Emma declared, "Her name is Nessie!"

BC, Charley and even Geppetto laughed. Cinderwan turned to the beast. "Is your name Nessie?" she asked.

The beast nodded. It spoke in a deep and melodious voice. "It fits," she said.

Cinderwan told the beast about Hansel's silly poem. A low rumble was heard. Its laugh reminded her of the laugh of the Earth Ancient.

10 An Impromptu Celebration

ews spread quickly across Oberland Kingdom that Queen Cinderella was coming home.

Everyone came to Alpine Lake to celebrate.

People gathered food for a celebration picnic and came to Alpine Lake. Water sprites from Hawaii flew there as well. They brought food for a picnic. Several students from Oberland School heard about lunch and flew with the dragons to join the party.

Gretel and Hansel walked out of the cave with the baby water beast. Red was wide-eyed. She had never seen so many people.

Geppetto's leg was better, and he walked about. Everyone mixed and talked.

Cinderwan was back to her regular size. She walked across the lake with Nessie. Thistle came over to hug them. She whispered to Cinderwan, "Congratulations, Cinderwan. Elders in training can be overwhelmed by 'righteous anger" when they gain the power of the Fire Element."

Cinderwan sighed and said, "that was close. I was prepared to put an end to Nessie."

Thistle smiled at her. "But you didn't."

Thistle came over to hug Cinderwan and Nessie.

Cinderwan suddenly realized something. "Nessie has done this before, hasn't she?"

"You *are* intuitive, aren't you?" smiled Thistle. "Looks can be deceiving. Nessie is like Pele. She is an Ancient, a manifestation of the Water Element. You will meet her again during your testing in another of her forms."

Cinderwan nodded. She looked at Nessie. Nessie smiled at her and winked. Thistle continued. "The Water Ancient has taken a great interest in your training. We have not trained a Five Element Master in living memory."

Cinderwan realized that the drama had been a field test before she could train with the Water Ancient.

A short distance away King Jorgan was talking with Charley, "I understand that you fought off Nessie when she was angry."

Charley nodded.

"That was brave of you," smiled Gretel.

King Jorgan asked, "Do you remember when you said you wanted to be a 'real boy'?"

Emma watched closely as Charley nodded. "I have grown up some," said Charley.

The king smiled at Charley and patted him on the back. "In many ways, Charley, you are much more than a boy."

Geppetto, Hansel, BC, and Papa Bear looked on as King Jorgan talked with Charley.

"In many ways, Charley, you are much more than a boy."

"Nice job, Pinocchio!" shouted Hansel.

"Okey!" he added, raising his hand.

"Dokey!" said BC, joining in and raising his hand.

"In the pokey!" shouted the three Billy Boys Gruff. They did a high five.

"Emma defended us too," added Gretel.

Sage turned to Emma. She looked at her red sparkles. She said, "And you, my dear, are still very connected to Zorcon".

Gretel winked at Emma and hugged her.

Sage continued, "Perhaps soon we will have some 'Billy Girls Gruff' too!"

Cinderwan looked to Nessie and Thistle. It would be best not to say anything about Nessie's true nature. That was Elder business. Facing everyone, she said "Nessie was worried that her baby might be harmed."

Then she bowed to Nessie. "I am sorry that it took me so long to understand the situation," she continued.

She looked to Thistle and the other Elders. "And I had a little help from my friends."

Geppetto said, "We did not understand either. We did not know that Red was in the cave."

The other girls watched on as the Elders talked with Emma.

Nessie nodded. Red joined her mother and nuzzled her.

"Water beasts normally live in the ocean," continued Cinderella. She turned to Thistle. "Unless I am mistaken, that is where we are going next." In her mind, Cinderwan suddenly saw herself in the ocean as a mermaid. Thistle was a whale. Nessie would take other forms.

The conversations continued into the afternoon. At one point, Emma turned to Gretel and asked, "May I ask you a question?"

Gretel was surprised. Conversations with Emma were mostly one-way. She would ask a question and Emma would answer it oddly. Emma *asking* a question was new. "Please do," answered Gretel.

Emma looked at her and asked, "Is this adventure what you meant by 'fun'?"

Thistle smiled. "Yes. We will go there soon with Nessie and Red."

Red nuzzled Nessie as the children looked on.

Gretel opened her mouth, but then shut it. She did not know what to say. The cave adventure had been a lot more than they had planned.

Cinderwan saw herself in the ocean as a mermaid.

Finally, she said, "This adventure was scary. But isn't little Red cute?" she added, looking at the baby water beast.

Emma nodded, "Perhaps it is the sort of thing where only later you realize it was fun."

11 Elder Council

he wind rustled as the Phoenix landed. The elders had gathered on a ledge overlooking the Great Mountain. Papa Bear, Mama Bear, Elder Eagle, Elder Coyote, and Wise Woman were already there.

"I see the light in you."

"I see the light in you," the Phoenix chirped. The meeting had begun.

Papa Bear bowed. "I see the light in you, Eldest Phoenix," he intoned. Turning to the other Elders, he continued. "I see the light in you, Elder Eagle of the Air Element. I see the light in you, Elder Mama Bear of the Fire Element. I see the light in you, Wise Woman of the Water Element. I see the light in you, Elder Coyote of Space and Time."

The Elders bowed and made their ritual greetings.

Then the Phoenix spoke again. "I requested this gathering to give thanks that balance has been restored."

Phoenix turned to Mama Bear. "With a little help from her friends, Cinderwan found her inner refuge."

Mama Bear nodded.

Coyote added, "I honor Mama Bear, who understood what was happening and assisted."

Mama Bear said, "I give thanks to Bodiwan, for guiding our newest Elder."

The Elders paused for a moment reflecting. Bodiwan was Cinderella's mother.

The Phoenix chirped, "We face chaotic times. Tiny events affect big ones. Bodiwan supported the continuation of this cycle."

Coyote continued. "Cinderwan temporarily lost her connection to the Stillness, the Silence, and the Spaciousness, but she found it in time. Her instincts are sound. She released her anger and supported life."

"Anger is one of the three distractions."

Turning to Coyote, the Phoenix added, "The mother guided the daughter. Cinderwan found her refuge. Then Cinderwan recognized and saved a mother and her child."

"Cinderwan is also with child," added Sage.

Mama Bear smiled.

Papa Bear cleared his throat and spoke, "Anger is one of the three distractions and clouds the mind."

The Elders nodded. They inhaled and then exhaled to dispel their own distractions.

Papa Bear continued. "Our community supports our journey."

He continued, "Coyote foresaw the arrival of the Zorconians."

Coyote nodded. A master of Space and Time, he had told them of his preparations. He said, "When change is coming, the Air Element is the first to move. I sense a wind from Zorcon even before Cinderwan trains in that element."

Elder Eagle spoke, "Cinderwan must next learn to fly and master the currents of the wind."

The elders nodded.

The Phoenix spoke softly, "Cinderwan's next test may be greater than the last."

12 Countdown on Zorcon

lder Coyote loped in the arcade at Zorcon University. In Oberland Kingdom, he had noticed a trail of red sparkles from Emma rising to the sky. The Zorconians had been observing Earth. It was time to return the attention.

Elder Coyote loped in the arcade at Zorcon University.

He created a space-time bubble. Coyote then followed the red nanobot sparkles to an orbiting Zorconian satellite around Earth and then though the wormhole. He then opened a portal to a space-time coordinate on the Zorcon University arcade where Professor Grimmicus had read a message from Emma.

Cameras recorded Coyote's sudden appearance. Coyotes had been extinct on Zorcon for thousands of years. The monitoring computers classified him as a Zorconian dog. Then they realized that there were no wild dogs on Zorcon.

The computers summoned animal control robots. It took a few minutes for the robots to reach the university arcade. By then the coyote had disappeared. The computers logged the observation as a probable system malfunction.

Grimmicus and the Oversight agents were in an orbital launch station, circling above Zorcon. The launching machinery adjusted launch parameters in preparation for the trip to Sol #3. A journey through a wormhole needed to be precise. The computers made delicate adjustments.

Grimmicus waited by the transfer train.

Grimmicus waited for the launch to be ready. He looked at the large disk-shaped starship through a viewport. A transport train would take them to the starship when it was ready.

His tablet signaled an alert from Marie's new appliance. The appliance reported that some children had named her "Emma". She had gone on a hike to "have fun" and report anomalies. She reported that a royal person, Queen Cinderella, had grown to a giant size and battled a water beast.

Grimmicus sighed. Really! This sort of nonsense sounded like earlier reports from Marie Gottmothercus. It was the stuff of fairy tales! The reporting included videos. Was the new android malfunctioning? What was happening on Sol #3?

The logs showed that the android had reconfigured her right arm into a titanium blade and struck a limb on the water beast! Grimmicus was surprised that an android would create and use a weapon. That seemed dangerous.

For an instant, Grimmicus thought that he saw a coyote. It hopped onto the table in front of him. In a flicker Elder Coyote became invisible. When Grimmicus looked again, the coyote was gone. Perhaps this folktale nonsense was affecting him. He shook his head.

Smithicus #1 and Smithicus #2 walked over to Grimmicus. The three of them were waiting to start a two-week journey to Sol #3. Grimmicus greeted them and spoke, "There may be cognitive tampering with Marie's new android."

For an instant, Grimmicus thought that he saw a coyote.

"According to the log on my tablet, Marie's new android reconfigured her metal arm into a sword and wielded it against a water beast. I hesitate to say it, but that seems both dangerous and *extraordinary*." Grimmicus emphasized the last word and raised an eyebrow.

Smithicus #2 said, "We saw the report."

Smithicus #1 shook his head. Then he said, "The deep neural networks in *all* of our androids have many cognitive layers and safeguards. These layers were developed for the earliest autonomous AI systems. The cyber-engineers realized that reliable protective instincts were needed to serve and protect humans. All appliances have these instincts. The android's defense was triggered when the water beast threatened the humans in the cave. Most people do not realize that androids will always try to defend them. In short," he concluded, "Emma's action was *ordinary*."

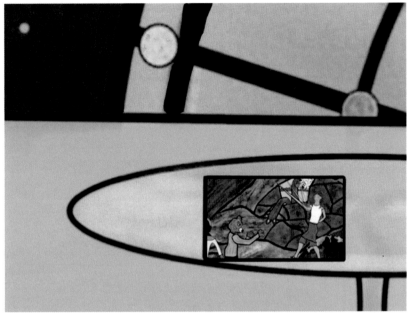

"They may have tampered with Marie's appliance."

Smithicus #1 added, "The defensive maneuver is not evidence of tampering at all. In fact, if the appliance *had not responded* to defend humans, *that* would be evidence of tampering."

Grimmicus grew thoughtful and nodded. "I did not know about that," he said. Apparently, there were things that none of them knew. Dangers could arise that none of them would expect.

Invisible to the three of them, Elder Coyote listened to the conversation carefully. Something was off about one of the two men talking with Grimmicus. Coyote focused his senses. Suddenly he noticed that Smithicus #1 was made largely of titanium, just like Charley. He had an outer layer of human-like skin.

Grimmicus did not know about the nature of this "man". The situation on Zorcon was more complex than Elder Coyote had expected.

Inwardly, Coyote saw that the starship had energy canons. The peaceful expedition included automated and armed backup. This starship might threaten Sol #3.

A door opened on the side of the transfer train. An automated announcement advised Grimmicus and the two Oversight agents to enter. It was time for the launch.

Smithicus #1 remarked, "In two weeks we will land on Sol #3 and start our expedition."

Smithicus #1 was largely titanium.

As the others took their seats, Coyote smiled. He would explore Zorcon and then return to Earth. Unlike the journey for the Zorconians in their starship, Elder Coyote's trip through a portal would take no time at all.

About the Author

Mark Stefik and his wife, Barbara Stefik, live in northern California. Mark is a computer scientist and inventor. Barbara is a transpersonal psychologist and researcher. They illustrate the stories together.

They can be contacted through their website at

www.PortolaPublishing.com

Made in the USA
Middletown, DE
30 April 2021